Katie and the Night Noises

by Jacqueline Sweeney · pictures by Arden Johnson

Troll Medallion

Library of Congress Cataloging-in-Publication Data

Sweeney, Jacqueline.
    Katie and the night noises / by Jacqueline Sweeney ; pictures by
Arden Johnson.
        p. cm.
    Summary: At bedtime, Katie has trouble going to sleep when all the
sounds in the house stir her imagination to hear sounds of the jungle.
    ISBN 0-8167-3014-8 (lib. bdg.) — ISBN 0-8167-3015-6 (pbk.)
    [1. Bedtime—Fiction. 2. Imagination—Fiction.] I. Johnson, Arden,
ill. II. Title.
PZ7.S974255Kat 1993
[E]—dc20   93-22198

It wasn't enough
to be tucked in tight by Mom each night.
Katie wanted more.

She wanted her cracker snack.

She wanted her closet closed
and her door cracked.

She wanted Doobie Bear sitting
on his wooden shelf.

She wanted the shell
of her seashell night light
facing out.

She wanted to clickity-click
her night light on
herself.

And she wanted to hear the motor-whir
of her Calico Kitty's purr.

And Katie wanted more.

She wanted a story
with pictures
of animals making loud sounds.

She wanted to hear fat hippos snort
and terrible tigers roar.
She wanted to close her eyes and hear
them in her mind.

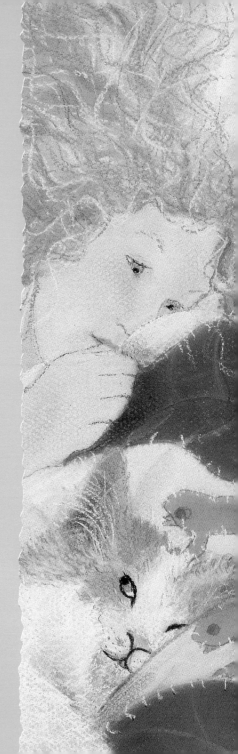

Instead,
Katie's mom picked stories
about frogs peeping sleep songs,
and breezes shushing leaves.

At bedtime
Mom liked to read about quiet things
making quiet sounds.

"It will help to calm you down,"
she said.

But Katie wanted more.

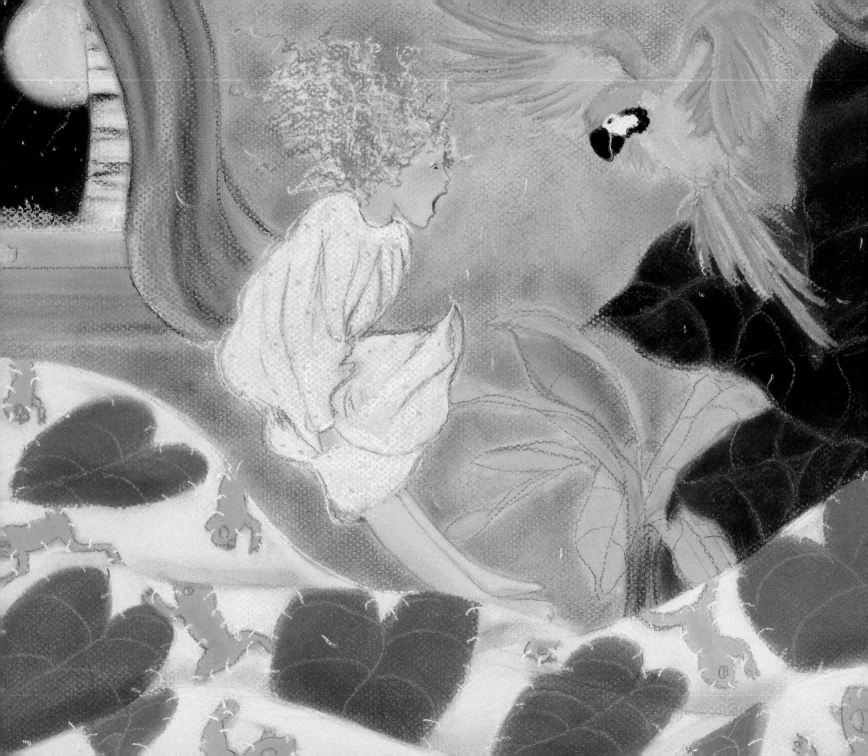

She wanted to stay awake LONGER
than ever before.
She closed her eyes.
She pretended to snore.

But as soon as her mother
was out the door,
Katie, Girl of the Jungle,
bounced from her bed to the floor.

She grabbed Doobie Bear
from his wooden shelf
and put on her big red hat.

Then Katie and Bear
started stalking the cat.

She leaped like a leopard
from floor to bed.
Bear growled like a lion
who hadn't been fed,

and Calico Kitty jumped straight in the air
from-the-bed-to-the-floor-through-the-
crack-in-the-door.

"What was that?" asked Mother.

"The cat," yelled Brother.

"KA—TIE!"
boomed the voice of her dad:

> "It's Nighttime
> Quiettime
> No time for Noisetime!"

Katie stood still as a tree trunk
beside her door.

She listened for elephant stomps
on the floor.

She listened with ape ears,
giraffe ears, and bat ears.

She listened much longer than ever before,

until out in the nighttime,
quiettime hall she heard
  HISS HISS
from the pipes in the wall,
and was sure that a jungle snake
eight feet long
had swallowed her brother
clothes and all.

But she heard no screams from the shower.

She heard SPLISHY-SPLASH!

SPLISHY-SPLASH!

WATERFALL!

Katie jumped when she heard

GURGLE-CRASH!

GURGLE-CLINK!

And although she heard
pans and plates in the sink,

she was sure
in the kitchen stood two big gazelles
gobbling supper
and dishes as well.

By now Kate felt wobbly
and crawled back to bed.

But she wanted to listen some more.

Outside her window:
a ghost-moaning wind——
a tree limb went TIPPY-TAP!
"Please let me in!"

She heard PLICKY-TICK!
PLICKY-TICK!
Sleet in the street,

and was sure that ten monkeys
with taps on their feet
were tap-dancing on rooftops and cars
and concrete.

Katie squeezed her eyes tight
and listened some more.
She listened much harder than ever before,

when something remarkable happened.

Her red hat grew feathers
and large, flapping wings
that lifted her to the night sky.

She flew over houses
and high over trees.

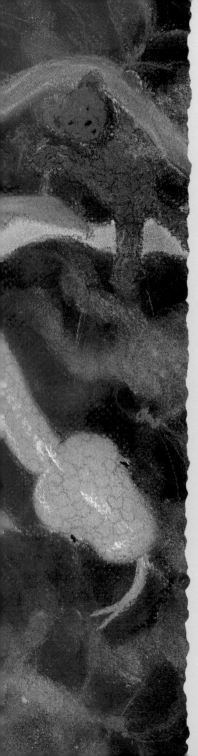

She flew fast past cities
and mountains and seas
'til she flip-flapped right into
the Jungle,

where Katie heard snakes hiss
and elephants scream.

She heard sounds from stories
her mom wouldn't read!

But she never heard SQUEAK
as her door opened wide.

She never heard Mom and Dad
tiptoe inside.

She never heard KISS
and she never heard HUG,
or their toes tiptoe softly
like mice through the rug.

She never heard Doobie
put back on his shelf,
or the click of the night light
she'd clicked on herself.

And she never heard the motor-whir
of Calico Kitty's purr.

For Katie was deep in her
Jungle of Dreams,
where all hippos snorted
and all tigers roared.

And Katie still wanted more…

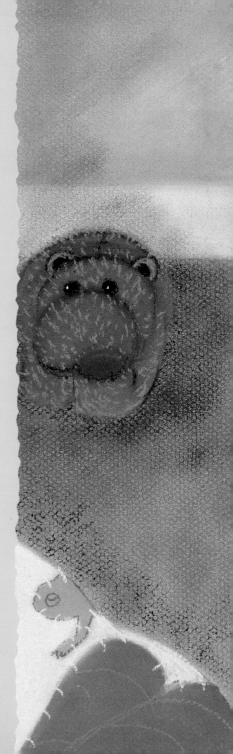